COPIOUS
AMOUNTSPRESS
and

ARDDEN

present

ANDREA GRANT'S

MINX

DREAM WAR

PUBLISHERS
**ANDREA GRANT / COPIOUS AMOUNTS PRESS
BRENDAN DENEEN, RICHARD EMMS / ARDDEN ENTERTAINMENT**

CREATOR / WRITER / MINX GALLERY COLLAGES
ANDREA GRANT

EDITOR
BRENDAN DENEEN

CONTRIBUTING EDITOR
CLAY THURMOND

ILLUSTRATION / COVERS
REY ARZENO

D1717042

INKER
ANNETTE TORRES

COLORISTS
PAPILLON STUDIO: AGUS YULIANTO, ANDY SAKURA, FAJAR BUANA

LETTERER
GINA MANISCALCO

STORY BY
ANDREA GRANT, GERRY JOBE & JESS BENNETT

GRAPHIC DESIGN
STEVE CASTRO

FOR MORE INFORMATION, PLEASE VISIT OUR WEBSITE:
WWW.COPIOUSAMOUNTS.COM

MINX COSTUME BY JESSICA CIARLA WWW.CIARLA.COM

**WE WISH TO ACKNOWLEDGE THE SUPPORT
OF THE CANADA COUNCIL FOR THE ARTS**   Canada Council
for the Arts

As an artist and storyteller, I've always approached any medium (photography, poetry, comics, what have you) as a collage. Memory forms the background of each work. Layers of literary and cultural references add texture. Experience works like scissors to cut those pieces into shreds. And tradition glues them all back together to form a picture.

Minx is a collage — spliced within these pages are my deepest memories, my obsessions, and my fears and desires, all bound together by my Native beliefs and culture. To know Minx is to know me, and to know me is to know that whatever Minx goes through, I've experienced in some way in my life.

I mean that allegorically for the most part, of course. But I actually do hold true the Native belief that when we sleep part of our consciousness travels to another dimension that might be just as valid as our waking reality. And the more we become aware of that, the more we are able to see the connections between those two worlds, with startling consequences.

Minx is the embodiment of that realization for me - through her, I am piecing together my own multi-layered history with the idea that someday, I will leave behind a whole picture. *Minx: Dream War* is the first part.

Andrea Grant
New York City, April 2, 2011

Afterdream
BY NIC KELMAN

Chuang Tzu tells a parable of a man who dreamed
he was a butterfly and after he awoke, from then on,
he was never sure if he was a butterfly
dreaming he was a man.

If there is one beautiful thing about Minx (and there
are many beautiful things about Minx), it is not that
dreams might be an alternate reality but that reality
might be an alternate dream. Nor is this simple
solipsism — there are many entities and forces outside
of Minx that act with their own will to pursue
their own desires. Rather it is a recognition that
consciousness is formed from within as much as from
without and that its creations are just as powerful as,
if not more powerful than, entities that exist outside it.

And what is art if not the belief that something that
comes from within us can be stronger than anything
that comes from without? So be aware as you turn
more of these pages that you will not be a reader,
but a dreamer. And dream on.

WHAT HAPPENED? WHERE AM I?

OH! I... I'M NOT AUTHORIZED TO ANSWER ANY QUESTIONS..

WELCOME BACK. HOW ARE YOU FEELING?

FINE, I GUESS.

WE'VE NOTIFIED YOUR EMERGENCY CONTACT. HE'LL BE HERE SHORTLY.

VIVIEN— YOU'RE AWAKE!

LIAM—WHAT HAPPENED LAST NIGHT?

LOOK, VIV... I.... UH... YOU'VE BEEN... UM...

WHAT? LIAM, YOU'RE SCARING ME.

YOU'VE BEEN IN A COMA. FOR A WHILE.

WHAT DO YOU MEAN? HOW LONG? WEEKS? MONTHS?

UM...

JUST SPIT IT OUT, LIAM!

SEVEN YEARS, VIV. YOU'VE BEEN IN A COMA FOR SEVEN YEARS.

YOUR PAINTING IS IMPROVING, SO NOW I'M GOING TO SHOW YOU HOW TO CARVE. THERE ARE SPIRIT FACES IN THE WOOD, SEE? THEY'LL TELL YOU WHAT PATTERNS TO MAKE.

OBJECTS HOLD SO MUCH MEMORY...

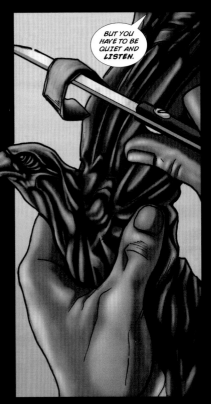

BUT YOU HAVE TO BE QUIET AND LISTEN.

DAD? IT'S VIV.

WHO?

YOUR DAUGHTER.

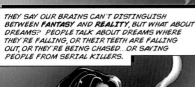

THEY SAY OUR BRAINS CAN'T DISTINGUISH BETWEEN *FANTASY* AND *REALITY*, BUT WHAT ABOUT DREAMS? PEOPLE TALK ABOUT DREAMS WHERE THEY'RE FALLING, OR THEIR TEETH ARE FALLING OUT, OR THEY'RE BEING CHASED...OR SAVING PEOPLE FROM SERIAL KILLERS.

SURE, THESE ARE ALL AWFUL SCENARIOS. BUT WHAT ABOUT THOSE FLASHES OF MEMORY THE DAY AFTER A NIGHTMARE, WHEN THAT DREAM IS STILL IN YOU LIKE A VIRUS?

MY DREAMS PHYSICALLY HURT. MY MUSCLES ARE STRAINED WHEN I WAKE UP, AS THOUGH I'M FIGHTING BATTLES EVERY NIGHT. THERE'S ALSO AN EMOTIONAL STRAIN FROM WATCHING PEOPLE I LOVE DIE, OVER AND OVER...

THE ONLY TIME I FEEL COMPLETE IS WHEN I PAINT – OR WHEN I HAVE A KNIFE IN MY HAND.

COAST SALISH ART IS ALL ABOUT JUXTAPOSITION: ANIMALS AND HUMANS CO-EXISITNG.

WE PORTRAY THAT THROUGH CIRCULAR SHAPES, CRESTS, AND TOTEMS. WHERE HUMANS LIVE INSIDE THE SKIN OF ANIMALS, OR ANIMALS LIVE INSIDE HUMANS.

WE BELIEVE OUR ANIMAL SPIRITS SURROUND AND PROTECT US, AND THEY TALK TO US AS MUCH AS THE SPIRITS IN THE WOOD WE CARVE.

WOW.

I'VE BEEN WORKING LIKE CRAZY—I THINK I HAVE ENOUGH WORK TO EXHIBIT NOW, RIGHT?

IT'S AMAZING! YOUR SHOW IS GOING TO SELL OUT.

TO BE CONTINUED...

Where do humans go when they dream?

THE EMPRESS

Does the soul leave the body and wander in another dimension?

There is an urban legend which claims if you die in DREAMTIME you'll not awaken in real life

THIS IS TRUE.

It's the reason the gods never

dare to slumber sound.

WE HAVE A LOT OF TIME ON OUR HANDS

You used to study Egyptology, Osiris and Isis, the Book of the Dead. You used to draw
hieroglyphics on my bare shoulders, running fingers over scars mapping my follicles.
Now you've put a hex on me & I don't feel human. The moon tides are running in my
blood – a wolf is rising up inside of me, skeletal lines shivering under honed muscle.

BONES

I am a sleepless metal shadow.

COPIOUS
AMOUNTSPRESS
and

ARDDEN

present

ANDREA GRANT'S

MINX

DREAM WAR

PUBLISHERS
**ANDREA GRANT / COPIOUS AMOUNTS PRESS
BRENDAN DENEEN, RICHARD EMMS / ARDDEN ENTERTAINMENT**

CREATOR / WRITER / DREAMTIME COLLAGES
ANDREA GRANT

EDITOR
BRENDAN DENEEN

CONTRIBUTING EDITOR
CLAY THURMOND

ILLUSTRATION / COVERS / INKING
REY ARZENO

COLORIST
PAPILLON STUDIO: AGUS YULIANTO

LETTERER
GINA MANISCALCO

STORY BY
ANDREA GRANT, GERRY JOBE & JESS BENNETT

GRAPHIC DESIGN
STEVE CASTRO

FOR MORE INFORMATION, PLEASE VISIT OUR WEBSITE:
WWW.COPIOUSAMOUNTS.COM

MINX COSTUME BY JESSICA CIARLA WWW.CIARLA.COM

**WE WISH TO ACKNOWLEDGE THE SUPPORT
OF THE CANADA COUNCIL FOR THE ARTS**

Canada Council
for the Arts

Foreward

By Justin Ridgeway

"How's Annie?"

This is the final line of David Lynch's *Twin Peaks*, a series that
explores, within the realms of the Black and White Lodges,
the nature and existence of Dopplegängers. Special Agent
Dale Cooper, it is revealed, as he speaks with a malicious
smirk to his mirror (itself a motif that symbolically reflects
the ontology of the double as a reversal of the original),
has been subsumed by his evil twin. This incarnation of the
Dopplegänger suggests that the other is inherently an opposite,
an inversion of the essential qualities of the primary,
and perhaps true, version of the self.

With the second issue of Minx we consider the Dopplegänger,
however, through a construction of another set of binaries
as represented by the worlds occupied in Dreamtime and
Wakingtime. The exploration is conducted across two
separate landscapes that are simultaneously metaphysical
and empirical (having a physical reality). This is a dialectical
system that positions both worlds as having truth and
consequences for each other; their effects register in both
domains; there is no singular reality other than that which
is constituted by the merging of the two. Similar to Wes
Craven's *Nightmare On Elm Street*, what happens in one world,
also is born in the other. This is something which Minx/Vivien
comes to realize: if you are wounded in Dreamtime, you will
bear the injury also in Wakingtime.

Vivien marvels at the purple skies and the cities that appear both modern and ancient in Dreamtime's world. For Vivien, this world is at first the unreal world, the alteration of reality. However, because both worlds have existence and therefore substance, Minx—as Vivien then becomes—must face the question: which world is the fantastical one? The familiar world of Wakingtime with its experiences that we come to apprehend consciously? Or the seemingly strange Dreamtime that we experience only when we enter the unconscious plane?

The answer—at least partially—is that the polarity is not defined as Real/Unreal, but, rather, Wake/Dream*. And between the two, only the thin veil of consciousness separates them.

The implication for Minx/Vivien is that while she is a singular being, she has two identities. The artist and the warrior. The woman who goes through her day then comes home to sleep in her apartment only to find herself battling the demons of her night-terrors, staving off those who would attempt to break through and break down the barriers that exist to protect the waking world from the chaos Ares intends. As you will see reading through the issue you have now in your hands, the task before Minx is daunting. The trial she faces in protecting one world from another is as fraught as the trial implicit in the reconciliation of her identities. One thing is certain, however: disruption will now become the constant in our heroine's life as she embarks on a quest that is crucial to finding her essential self.

* That said, if we consider Lacan, we can combine the two sets:
Real (Conscious) / Imaginary (Unconscious).

THEN EXPLAIN YOUR ART IF NONE OF THIS REALLY EXISTS. THAT CASTLE, THE SHAPE OF THE MOUNTAINS BEHIND IT. YOU KNOW THIS LANDSCAPE. THAT'S THE NIGHTMARE FOREST, WHERE WE USED TO HUNT. SEE THAT MOUNTAIN WITH ALL THE FACES IN IT? THAT'S IN A LOT OF YOUR PAINTINGS.

THIS CAN'T BE REAL.

THIS IS WHERE I LIVE. COME ON, I WANT TO SHOW YOU SOMETHING.

REMEMBER THIS PAINTING FROM YOUR SHOW? I WAS QUITE TAKEN WITH IT, AND DECIDED I HAD TO HAVE IT.

IMPOSSIBLE, I KNOW FOR A FACT THAT PIECE DIDN'T SELL.

IT DIDN'T SELL, BUT IT'S HERE NONETHELESS — NOT HANGING IN THE GALLERY.

HOW IS THIS POSSIBLE?

SOME PEOPLE ARE POWERFUL ENOUGH TO MOVE OBJECTS FROM THE WAKING WORLD INTO DREAMTIME.

EXCELLENT WORK. BUT IT'S TIME FOR YOU TO GO BACK TO THE WAKING WORLD NOW...

ALL OF A SUDDEN, I WAS BACK IN MY APARTMENT, DRESSED IN DIFFERENT CLOTHES THAN WHAT I'D FALLEN ASLEEP IN. WITH THAT PHYSICAL PROOF, I REALIZED IT WAS TRUE – DREAMTIME WAS A REAL PLACE.

I REMEMBERED EVERYTHING – THE PURPLE SKIES, CASTLES, AND THICK FORESTS, AND THE EMPRESS, WHO RULED HER DOMINION WITH A FIRM HAND. I REALIZED THAT PTOLEMY WAS THE REASON I WAS SO COMFORTABLE WIELDING A SWORD, BECAUSE WE'D FOUGHT SIDE BY SIDE IN BATTLE.

YES?

IT'S PTOLEMY.

YOU REMEMBER.

YES... I WOKE UP. AND IT WAS ALL SO CLEAR.

THE UNTAPPED LEY LINES ARE THE ONES THAT NATIVES HAVE KEPT SECRET. BUT ARES WANTS TO CONTROL THEM. HE'S BEEN HUNTING DOWN THE NATIVES IN THE HOPE OF FINDING THE KEY TO THEIR POWER.

ARES...YOU MEAN THE GOD OF WAR?

THAT'S HIM. HE'S THE LEADER OF THOSE HORRIBLE CREATURES WHO ALWAYS TRY TO HUNT YOU.

WHEN YOU CAME TO ME IN THE COMA, I SAW THAT YOU WERE THE ONLY ONE WHO COULD SERVE AS A GUARDIAN TO THE NATIVES IN DREAMTIME. THAT'S WHY ARES WANTS YOU DEAD.

COME. I HAVE A GIFT FOR YOU.

YOU'LL NEED TO PROTECT YOURSELF.

THANK YOU, EMPRESS.

AND YOU CAN CALL THE WOLVES FORTH WITH YOUR AMULET, IF YOU NEED BACK-UP.

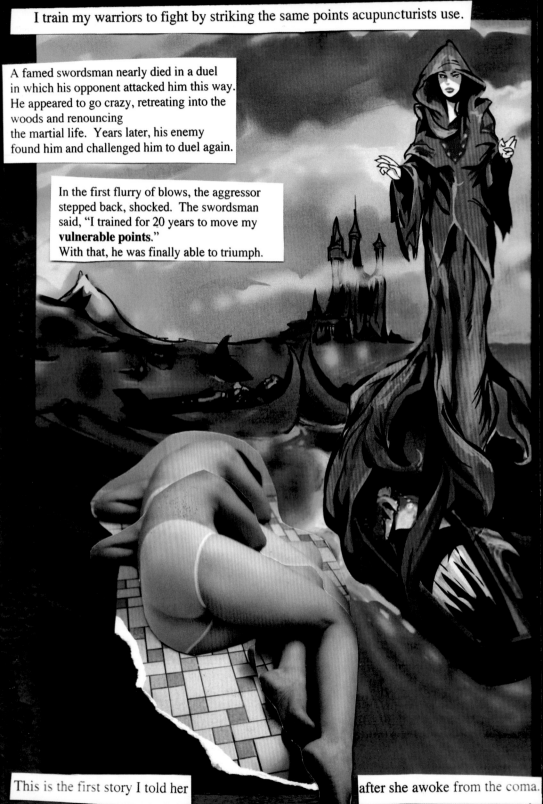

I train my warriors to fight by striking the same points acupuncturists use.

A famed swordsman nearly died in a duel
in which his opponent attacked him this way.
He appeared to go crazy, retreating into the
woods and renouncing
the martial life. Years later, his enemy
found him and challenged him to duel again.

In the first flurry of blows, the aggressor
stepped back, shocked. The swordsman
said, "I trained for 20 years to move my
vulnerable points."
With that, he was finally able to triumph.

This is the first story I told her   after she awoke from the coma.

MINX

ANDREA GRANT'S

COPIOUS AMOUNTSPRESS *and*
ARDDEN *present*

DREAM WAR

PUBLISHERS
ANDREA GRANT / COPIOUS AMOUNTS PRESS
BRENDAN DENEEN, RICHARD EMMS / ARDDEN ENTERTAINMENT

CREATOR / WRITER / DREAMTIME COLLAGES
ANDREA GRANT

EDITOR
BRENDAN DENEEN

CONTRIBUTING EDITOR
CLAY THURMOND

COVER
REY ARZENO

ILLUSTRATION/INKING
MIKE WILLIAMS

COLORIST
PAPILLON STUDIO: ANANG SETYAWAN

LETTERER
GINA MANISCALCO

PTOLEMY SPEAKS SHORT STORY
PREVAIL

STORY BY
ANDREA GRANT, GERRY JOBE & JESS BENNETT

GRAPHIC DESIGN
STEVE CASTRO

FOR MORE INFORMATION, PLEASE VISIT OUR WEBSITE:
WWW.COPIOUSAMOUNTS.COM

MINX COSTUME BY JESSICA CIARLA WWW.CIARLA.COM

WE WISH TO ACKNOWLEDGE THE SUPPORT
OF THE CANADA COUNCIL FOR THE ARTS
 Canada Council
for the Arts

Foreward
by Paul Seesequasis

Minx is a woman between worlds. In one world there is the bustling, seductive metropolis of today's New York City with all its fascinations and dangers, and then there is another world of Dream-time where myth and legends persist and things are truly not what they seem. Minx is a modern young woman, beautiful, intelligent, and strong - but she is also haunted, troubled and caught between two often conflicting worlds.

As a mixed-blood Native American, Minx cannot help but hear the echoes of her Native ancestry. Her bloodline, through her father, courses through her veins and within it wields the power that she must unlock if she is to fulfill her destiny and save her people.

The streets of Manhattan seem a far cry from the world of ancient spirits, tortured ghosts, and whispered prophecies, but they are there in the streets nonetheless, if only she is able to hear them. It is a city that never sleeps but that does not mean that the dreams do not haunt her. She has her own prophetic vision. Her own road she must follow.

It takes a moment of extreme danger, of being on the precipice of falling permanently into the spirit world, to awaken this power within her. For many Native Americans, this sadly is often the case. The powers lie untapped. The potential is wasted. The burden of history too great. The barriers too formidable to overcome. It takes a crisis to bring the change. Minx is remarkable in this way. She is a woman able to survive to dig into strengths that are super-human. But for her to do so, she must also be accepting of the ancestral voice within her. It is not always easy. Visions that change the world seldom are.

The animal spirits dwell within her. They are the bridge Minx must cross to channel her powers. In Dream-time the packs of white wolves roam down the avenues, the eagle spirits soar over the Chrysler Building and the mythical bear saunters down the darkened alleyways. But it is not enough for her to simply turn them on. She must learn to harness them, to interpret and listen and accept that they contain great mysteries and powers that even the wisest Shaman can never fully comprehend.

The best stories written are often those that we dig deep within ourselves to release. Most writers accept this. In reading Andrea Grant's *Minx* comic series I cannot help but feel she has dug deep within herself to release this. I applaud her, as this series is unique, well crafted, expertly drawn, and needed. I hope its readers will develop a new curiousity about Native American beliefs and decide to delve further into them. I hope they realise that the ancient myths and stories of Native America have a deep resonance and meaning to our own challenging times.

I also desire that Andrea Grant will build a readership among Native Americans - in particular those with the mixed-blood experience. We walk within two worlds and that is not always easy. But it can be a gift that allows one to see what others don't. We see this with Minx.

Yes Minx is often in danger and faces many conflicts. Without conflict there is no story. And, it is only with conflict and challenge that she can grow stronger. Her ancestral gift is the weapon to help her survive. Andrea Grant has tapped into her past to open a powerful present. Minx is a woman of today - vibrant, sexy, powerful, and imbued with a Native American spirit - and I know of no other comic heroine like her.

Thank you, Andrea, for this creation.

Paul Seesequasis is the author of Tobacco Wars, *"The Republic of Tricksterism", and numerous other fictions. He is currently working on a new novel.*

TO BE CONTINUED...

Ptolemy Speaks...
by Prevail

My tainted legacy began from the purest of intents: the deep love between two people. Yet, even in the womb, the strings of destiny were being woven. The strength and enduring power of my parents was felt by the world, and their union would bear children of great ambition. My Father, Mark Antony, was one of the most heralded Generals in the bloodied history of warfare. It was rumored when he rode into battle mounted upon a steed clad in armor and the gold crest of Caesar's Legion, my Father could make entire front lines retreat from the brazen look of victory that consumed his eyes. Some had described it as the fire of Hades and, indeed, many did burn once within its swirling inferno. My Mother, the legendary Queen of Egypt, possessed a beauty so unmatched that men and woman alike were known to openly weep in her presence. Even with all the grace and distinguishability of my parents' union, there was despair on the horizon, and soon enough the Empire would be shaken.

I was born into war. A campaign against the dreaded Octavian had run the Jewel of the Nile into insurmountable peril. As a youth, The Royal Scholars versed me well in the ancient Greek that dotted my lineage, as well as introducing me to the keys of unlocking the wonders of the Egyptian language. Although we were separated by years, there was nothing that could cause a gap between myself and my twin siblings. Our bond was innate and unspoken. As my eldest brother and I grew in age, so grew our competitiveness. In all things recreational and scholastic, our respectful one-ups-manship became our cornerstone, with the older children teaching the younger and occasionally, the other way around. Our dear sister was blossoming as a beautiful flower, and the Court Maidens were sure to keep her access to the populace limited and brief. Then, in one swift instance, the innocence of our youth was taken from us.

On a fateful September day, my Father, The Great Mark Antony, was defeated by Octavian in the Battle of Actium. This loss, a true anomaly on my Father's indisputable record of engagements, stung him deeply, as if a furious honey bee, aware of its signal dose of potency, were trapped in a corner by a predator, his poison still inflicting injury, yet his inevitable death self-administered. When my Father returned home he was still a deadly bee, but all his breadth of intimidation and infliction had been usurped. What came next sparked a chain of events that led to my present state.

Unable to face the loss at the hands of his hated foe, my Father, a now broken shell of a man, drank himself into discontent and proceeded to plunge a lengthy dagger of the Roman military deep into his abdomen. Never will my mind erase this memory. I remember watching the red spill from his body, as though a vat of precious wine had been pierced by the elephant tusk and left to drain its entirety in solace. Soon enough the next link in the chain of events would break. After months of heartbreak and millions of teardrops, my Mother, the enviable Cleopatra, followed suit in my Father's footsteps, and tradition took its course. The Pharaoh Queen had her maidens draw her evening bath, a soothing mixture of warmed milk and gold dust. But on this night an ornately woven basket was presented by her washing basin, its contents alive enough to bring certain death. On request of her most trusted servant, my Mother ask that the reed vestibule be gently tipped, allowing its venomous inhabitant to find home in the mercurial bath. One clasping of the viper's mandible and the deadly inoculation would be instantly historic. The symbol that once adorned the crown of my family's Empire had come to manifest itself as a false protector, even the Eagle that once represented my Father's prowess had been victim to the snake's bite.

In the days to follow, doom and despair would reacquaint themselves with my bloodline. The armies of Octavian, now hoisting victory laurels, marched upon our beloved Egypt and forever changed all we had known. I wept silently at night as I watched our great libraries smolder in the near distance, their singed outlines looking like a Phoenix whose magnificent life had come to a cyclic end, never to be reborn the same as in its former glory. The chamber doors to my eldest brother's room were battered down. He made a last-minute attempt to die honorably under the curvature of the same blade that had taken our Father's life, but the soldiers of Octavian were overly punctual and prevented him from his task. Instead, they wrangled him by the back of his dark chestnut hair and held him in a way that left his neck exposed. My sister and I were forced to watch as a sharp stiletto was plunged into our brother's throat, relinquishing it of air. We were wise enough to not show any remorse, even a gasp of shock would have meant we were next, and the importance of our survival was now paramount.

My sister and I were disjoined soon afterwards. Discarded between two Roman families that shared sympathies with the Republic, my dear sister and I were raised in the shackles of Octavian's vision. Quick to humiliate my sister and me as the "last survivors of a Dynastic enemy," our new suitor was also bold enough to carry a locket of our dead brother's hair in a leather pouch, which he wore around his neck as a reminder of his conquest. Upon first sight of this, I was filled with rage and vowed revenge for our entire family.

Being careful to never show my contempt or hatred toward Octavian, I finally reached my 17th birthday. Allowed to embark on a journey of character-building manhood, I sequestered a small caravan of other local young men-to-be, and we departed for the hills of Greece. As night fell and the fire reached its wavering hands towards the Heavens, I made my escape. In two days, I had reached my destination—the Temple of Ares. In my heart, I had known this ancient God had always shown my Father favor and was confident he would bestow upon me the tools for revenge.

For countless hours I lay on the dirt floor of the God of War's temple. Not sobbing, not showing remorse, but expressing the deepest hatred my soul could conjure. Then, like a golden bugle waking the forces of an unstoppable army, music attacked my ears and heart. The voice that followed was darker than abyss:

"Rise now," came the words, as if yelled by a million men from a mile away. And when I took to my feet, I was instructed to disclose the source of my discontented malice. My jaws drew open and the following words of eternal regret ushered themselves forth.

"God Ares, I am Ptolemy. I take this name, adopted from my long lost brother, who was wronged at the hands of the evil Octavian. I hereby swear my undying allegiance to you, my Lord, if only you grant me the means to avenge my family and restore our namesake!"

The grounds of the Temple shook with violence. I shrank into a ball in anticipation of the walls following suit, but nothing, except the booming voice again, this time it's temperament less foreboding.

"Ptolemy, know this and this alone. I will grant you the means to defeat this Octavian, but your sacrifice will be ultimate!" Upon those last words, not just the ground or Temple walls shook; the entire world buckled. Again, the booming sentiment of the God of War echoed, "It would seem your plight has found a soft spot in the rigidness of my wife's callous exterior. The mighty Aphrodite has convinced me to bestow you with a host of attributes, the least of which not being your newly appointed handsomeness and a certain charm that will make women bend to your every desire!"

was enraged. I could not kill Octavian with a simple smile and a bit of boyish charm. I wanted strength and revenge, certain and incontestable death for my rival. Ares had heard my internal strife and answered without verbal confirmation. Instead, he gave me all the physical and immortal instruments one could ever ask for. I felt my mind change, my body, too. Both felt like a strong red lantern glowing with an endless fuel, yet instead of confusion, I felt pure calm. The blood in my veins changed color. My brain was connected to all things, alive and inanimate. I felt for my face. Its structure had also been reborn, more rigid and distinguished. A last, omnipotent voice shot down upon me, although this time it was graced with the cadence of a woman who spoke with a sense of warning.

No woman will refuse you, and no man will dare stand against your will. But for those who know the ancient ways...well, you had best avoid them." With these words I fell into a deep sleep.

I awoke again in a pool of blood. My first visions were a blend of my Father's death and the still body of my Mother surrounded by milk and venom. As my neck craned upward, I beheld the corpse of Octavian, all his vital life granting fluids dashed upon the wall like a rugged painting. In one hand, the same dagger my Father had used to take his own life, in the other, the limp scaly dimensions of a venomous asp, its frail body plump with death. I knew instantly what I had done, what I had succeeded in doing. Grandeur and immortality were now mine, the sweet taste of revenge rolled across my tongue.

As centuries passed, I grew bored. All the killing on behalf of Ares did not stir my emotion. I walked and floated through time as a shadow, and many moons passed until I felt a rift in this plane—a rift that caused my excitement and piqued my curiosity. I have experienced an energy equal to mine, albeit more pure in intent and its effect is all-consuming. It would seem the Oracle of Delphi's prediction has rung true: the rise of a forceful opponent has begun its journey, and I may, at last, be charged with the grandest rivalry of my existence. In a strange way, I am certain our roles will become tangled in trying to protect and destroy each other all at once. But to relinquish any of my powerful grasp is not in my nature yet. I can foresee that this woman will test me for it, and I anticipate an epic battle to ensue. The thoughts of rivalry consume me from within. I feel the presence of the one known as Minx and welcome our doubtless contests. I only hope that to one of us, it brings final salvation.

ANDREA GRANT'S

PUBLISHERS
ANDREA GRANT / COPIOUS AMOUNTS PRESS
BRENDAN DENEEN, RICHARD EMMS / ARDDEN ENTERTAINMENT

CREATOR / WRITER / DREAMTIME COLLAGES
ANDREA GRANT

EDITOR
BRENDAN DENEEN

CONTRIBUTING EDITOR
CLAY THURMOND

ILLUSTRATION/INKING
MIKE WILLIAMS & REY ARZENO (Cover, Page 11 & 12)

COLORIST
PAPILLON STUDIO: ANANG SETYAWAN, FAJAR BUANA, AND BURHAN ARIF

LETTERER
GINA MANISCALCO

SKETCH
DAVID MACK

STORY BY
ANDREA GRANT, GERRY JOBE & JESS BENNETT

GRAPHIC DESIGN
STEVE CASTRO

FOR MORE INFORMATION, PLEASE VISIT OUR WEBSITE:
WWW.COPIOUSAMOUNTS.COM

MINX COSTUME BY JESSICA CIARLA WWW.CIARLA.COM

**WE WISH TO ACKNOWLEDGE THE SUPPORT
OF THE CANADA COUNCIL FOR THE ARTS**

Canada Council
for the Arts

Foreward
by Nanette Maxim

...we wake up electrified out of the coma by our own souls' airplanes roaring over the roof...
— Allen Ginsberg, "Howl"

Howl.

It starts low in the throat, mournful, then rises, pitching to a crescendo of high-lonesome yearning. When the wolf howls, the still veil of night is momentarily lifted, and another world is revealed.

For Native peoples, the wolf symbolizes loyalty and wisdom, fierceness and pride. That the wolf is Viven's totem, her protector as she walks between the worlds of Dreamtime and Waking, makes us cock our ears to hear her echo its call.

Through the first three issues of Andrea Grant's modern myth, we've witnessed the Waking Vivien turn her high-lonesome New Yorker into Dreamtime warrior Minx, the defender of her Coast Salish ancestors and of the family that's slipped from her grasp. Her growing howl reclaims her power, as she becomes, not just a bearer of the totem, but the alpha of the wolf pack that is ever reflected in the pools of her eyes.

For Minx, the call of the wild has grown deafening; it's a cry she can no longer ignore. Knives out. Game on.

In the best tradition of the graphically told story, it's a battle within our heroine mirroring a world, literally, in the balance. But that's not to say that traveling with Minx as she's embarked on this very strange trip has been all serious business. Along the way, we've cocktailed with the Oracle of Delphi, locked lips with a dreadlocked Greek hero, encountered a scarlet-cloaked Empress as enticing and possibly wicked as any sorceress from the Brothers Grimm. In Minx's struggle with Ares, the very modern god of war, she's spirited to the Dreamtime on the god's motorcycle, conjuring images of Jean Cocteau's take on the Orpheus myth, in which the henchmen of death lead their victims to the underworld on high-pitched motos.

Did we just hear that wolf pack growl? Betrayal awaits behind every dangerous curve (including her own), and in her journey, where the slippery duality of her existence begins to morph into a whole, this far-from-fragile sleeping beauty must face down her own greatest fears, at times battling her most entrenched instincts, born of love and loss.

As Andrea has given her alter ego life and words, so pencillers Rey Arzeno and Mike Williams, along with the brilliant colorists and letterers, have created a Minx as magnetic as those metaphysical ley lines, the forces of energy that are the force of our heroine's destiny.

Travel now with this weaver of dreams. Hear her howl.

From childhood, I've had trouble sleeping, staying up until 5 or 6 in the morning, as though I needed the cold reality of daylight to soothe me.
The monsters are not as frightening when you can see them clearly.

My nightmares are vivid paroxysms of blood & death. I don't know how to draw the line between dreams & reality.

Native Americans believe that when we dream we go into another dimension. I know this. Every day I wake up exhausted, with burning muscles, as though I have fought a tremendous battle.

Often, I am fighting myself. There is something primal living under my skin. There is a slow burning rage & a sense of urgency.

I've always had trouble sleeping

And sometimes I can't wake up.

We gods are misunderstood. We tell our stories in riddles; from the crystalline skies we watch the game of humans...their trivialities, agonies, ecstasies...death and rebirth. Humans call it meddlesome, but they still play along.

In desperate moments they seek our advice.

THERE IS POWER IN SYMBOLS.

Praying to stone gods.

The runes.

The tarot deck.

Symbols = archetypes.

Metaphor is everywhere.

We watch WAKESLEEP

with interest.

Sometimes we do interfere...

but we prefer to stay in the realm of the sleeping.

In WAKESLEEP, there has always been a human need for salvation. Every generation has had leaders who come forward to accept the responsibility.

DO YOU THINK YOU'RE CLEVER, RAISING THE DEAD?! AS THOUGH A PHANTOM ARMY IS AS POWERFUL AS THE GOD OF WAR?!

MINX, YOUR TOTEMS ARE OUT OF REACH, AND IN THE END, I'M A STRONG OPPONENT...

GRANDFATHER!

Minx: Dream War Biographies

Andrea Grant
Creator/Writer/Dreamtime Collage Artist

Minx: Dream War is the first in a graphic novel series that deftly blends the folklore of Andrea Grant's own Native American heritage with Greek mythology, Taoist philosophy and the classic archetypes developed by Joseph Campbell. The result is a work that explores the power of legend and myth–while also being a dizzying, ur-realist adventure. It finds Grant carrying on the tradition of her people, using comics as a way of preserving the old myths and narratives of her heritage in a contemporary format. "In a lot of ways, the current shift from the print to the digital medium reminds me of how so many First Nation stories got lost in the transition from oral history to print," Grant says. "There's an urgent need right now to share those narratives with the world in a contemporary, accessible format."

In that way, *Minx* is also Grant's own story, a kind of allegory that mirrors her own passage out of darkness into a greater discovery of both herself and her history. Her accomplishments are many and diverse: in 2001, she began the 'zine *Copious* as a showcase for her poetry; over the years, it's evolved to become an all-encompassing web publication featuring original writing, photography and artwork. She's a respected model and an adventurous artist, one who blends photography with poetry and sound recordings to create immersive, multi-dimensional work.

In 2009, she published *The Pin-Up Poet* through her own Copious Amounts Press, a book that pairs noirish photos of Grant, portraying a number of different characters, with imagistic poetry that offers insight into the women's identities or predicaments.

But as accomplished as this resume is, like the protagonist of *Minx*, it took Grant a long time to unlock her inner life. Born in Vancouver into a family of Jehovah's Witnesses, Grant found herself growing increasingly wary of the church's teachings, a skepticism that grew deeper as her father began to explore his own lineage. "My father began rediscovering his Native roots later in life," she explains. "He left the religion and had a kind of shamanistic breakdown, and he remembered things that his father had taught him as a kid, which filtered down to me."

Grant eventually left both the religion and the Pacific Northwest, relocating to New York to concentrate on her art. The concept for Minx developed over a period of several years (the name appears as an alias as early as a 2001 issue of Grant's 'zine *Copious*), gradually expanding to include roles for many of Grant's friends, and to draw a greater level of focus on "Dreamtime"–the parallel dimension Vivian–who will later rediscover her identity as the superheroine Minx–visits while she is asleep.

That concept also comes from Grant's past: Native Americans believe that when you sleep, you actually visit a world just as rich as the one you inhabit while awake. Vivian's identity in Dreamtime–and what it is she has to accomplish while she's there–will be revealed over the course of the next several books. Throughout, Grant expands on the notions of heritage, personal choice and identity, using Vivien/Minx's adventures as a way to explore the notion of loyalty to one's tribe, and being true to your past while confronting the obstacles that lie ahead.

"What I hope is interesting about Minx is that the characters are flawed *humans* struggling to find their own path," Grant says. "So they might care about each other, and they might connect with each other, but when things are dire, they might also betray each other. I think there are some elements that aren't typical of comic-book storytelling, but which are prevalent in Aboriginal legends."

Minx spikes a thoughtful consideration of mythology with moments of bone-chilling suspense–Grant's admitted love of Neil Gaiman's *Sandman* and Joe Linsner's *Dawn* can be felt in many of its vivid passages–but ultimately it is about one woman's journey, both across dimensions and into her own past.

"A lot of this is about returning to tribe, remembering where you're from," Grant explains. "It's about going back and revisiting your familial origins, and realizing the larger scope of why you end up somewhere mythologically."

"Mythology is portrayed in a lot of comics," Grant explains. "But I hope when people read *Minx* they also get a sense of the modern Native. Outside of Sherman Alexie, there aren't a whole lot of writers who are sharing the contemporary struggles of Native people. I wanted to use *Minx* to show how racial identity, and the day-to-day culture of Native people, is more complicated than the stereotypes we've all grown up with."

And, in reading about Vivian, Grant hopes perhaps people can find a bit more of themselves. "I'd like in some way to inspire people," she says, "and to show that if you follow your own path, there's a redemption."

Ardden Entertainment: Brendan Deneen and Richard Emms
Co-Publishers
Founded in 2008, Ardden Entertainment is the proud publisher of *Flash Gordon, Casper the Friendly Ghost*, and the ATLAS Comics resurrection, among others. Ardden is run by former Miramax Films executive Brendan Deneen (who also edited *Minx: Dream War*) and comic-book-store owner Richard Emms, with industry legend Mike Grell acting as the company's Editor-in-Chief. Ardden's goal is to produce high quality licensed comic books as well as original concepts that work both as comic books and larger, multi-media properties. For more information about Ardden Entertainment, please visit www.Ardden-Entertainment.com.

Rey Arzeno
Illustrator Part 1 & 2/Cover Artist
Rey made his first comic convention appearance at New York Comic Con in 2009 alongside Drumfish Productions as colorist for their book, *Neverminds*. It was at this convention he met Andrea Grant, the writer of *Minx*. It would be the first time his line work would be published. The first issue hit shelves May 25th; which was the birthday of Rey's dearly departed Mother; making it's release not just a milestone, but a dedication.

Papillon Studio has been working on the creation of comic books and other illustration projects since the year 2002. The team members were all born in Semarang, the capital of Central Java, Indonesia. Papillon's talented artists enjoy turning creator/writer's ideas into exciting sequential pages, covers, pinups, and character designs, using both digital coloring and traditional illustration.

Gina Maniscalco
Letters

Gina Maniscalco lives in Brooklyn, New York, and is currently the Senior Designer at *DETAILS* Magazine. She enjoys binding her own books and is an active member of the Society of Publication Designers. She's into traveling and riding her bike, spending as much time outside as possible.

Steve Castro
Graphic Design

Steve Castro is a print and web designer, who has previously worked on projects for WWE, UFC, Universal Studios, MGM, as well as many local companies in the New York area.

Way back in 2006, Steve answered a MySpace(!) post looking for a web designer, and has been working with Andrea on Minx ever since.

Steve currently resides on Long Island with his wife and two children. He enjoys cooking, Knicks games, movies and, of course, comics.

Acknowledgements...

George Orwell once said, "Writing a book is a horrible, exhausting struggle, like a long bout of some painful illness. One would never undertake such a thing if one were not driven by some demon whom one can neither resist nor understand." This is true. *Minx: Dream War* took an army to create, and I am grateful to have had such talented allies along the way.

Firstly, thank you to Rey, Mike, Alfa and the colorists at Papillon Studio for the painstaking artwork that brings this story to life the way I've always envisioned it in my brain, purple Dreamtime skies and all. To Brendan Deneen and Richard Emms at Ardden, my co-publishers who have provided constant enthusiasm and support. To Steve Castro, the most patient of graphic designers, who has helped brand *Minx* in a glorious way from day one.

Thank you to Gerry Jobe and Jess Bennett, for working with me on story concepts throughout the years, and to my original comic book gang for the lessons they taught me along the way: Christian Beranek, Rich Bernatovech, and Philip Clark. To Joe Linsner, Jim Saliscrup, and David Mack for being mentors, perhaps unwittingly.

Thanks to my colleagues at *DETAILS* Magazine, Clay Thurmond and Gina Maniscalco, for your respective copy editing and lettering talents.

Thanks to Jessica Ciarla, for designing the Minx costume, and thereby answering the question "What would a girl living in New York wear if she was called to an epic superhero adventure?"

Thanks to Sarah Keenlyside, for keeping her sharp eye upon my aesthetic and reminding me of my Vancouver Island origins. To Nic Kelman, Justin Ridgeway, Paul Seequasis, and Nanette Maxim for powerful introductions to every episode of *Dream War*.

To my family, for honoring traditional Coast Salish legends, and for encouraging me to pursue the arts. To my friends, who allowed me to exploit their likenesses in the form of comic characters, posing for many reference photographs along the way, sometimes in costume: Prevail (Ptolemy), Candice Pitcher (the Empress), Teri Munro (Rhiannon), Paul Barnla (Dez), and to the friends who always had my back in the darkest hours of creation (Jennifer McClain, Ziya Tong, Carolyn Lair).

Thanks to Olga Nemcova and Alexandra Tavel of October Anniversary for working with me to create the "Wolf Charm" jewelry. To Emily Inverso, for assisting me with all sorts of organizational things on this project. Thanks to my public relations divas who are about to unleash their powers in taking this project to the masses, Dawn Kamerling and Malania Dela Cruz.

Lastly, thanks to the Canada Council, who made all of this possible. And, of course, to my fans, for appreciating.

See you in Dreamtime...

-Andrea Grant